DOCTOR SQUASH
The Doll Doctor

Published in the United States by Golden Books, an imprint of Random House Children's Books,
a division of Random House, Inc., 1745 Broadway, New York, NY 10019. Originally published
with different illustrations in the United States by Simon and Schuster, Inc., and
Artists and Writers Guild, Inc., in 1951. Golden Books, A Golden Book, and the G colophon
are registered trademarks of Random House, Inc.
www.randomhouse.com/kids
Educators and librarians, for a variety of teaching tools, visit us at www.randomhouse.com/teachers
Library of Congress Control Number: 2007937897
ISBN: 978-0-375-84800-1 (trade)—978-0-375-95623-2 (lib. bdg.)
PRINTED IN CHINA
10 9 8 7 6 5 4 3 2 1

DOCTOR SQUASH
The Doll Doctor

by Margaret Wise Brown

illustrations by David Hitch

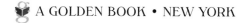 A GOLDEN BOOK · NEW YORK

The poor little Wooden Soldier was sick,
so sick he squeaked,
  "Mother, Mother, I am sick
  Call for the Doctor, quick, quick, quick."
  So the other dolls put him to bed and they
called for Doctor Squash, the Doll Doctor.

Doctor Squash came running with his little bag. He opened his bag and took out a spoon and a bottle, and a stethoscope to listen to the little Wooden Soldier's heart.

Of course, dolls have no hearts, and Doctor Squash knew this. But he pretended they did have hearts, because it made the dolls feel better.

"Poor old thing," said Doctor Squash, "you need oil. You are positively squeaky."

So Doctor Squash gave the little squeaky doll some oil of cherry and some oil of plum in a silver spoon, right down his squeaky little throat.

And he left some honey and amber cough drops in case the little Soldier coughed. But he didn't. So all the dolls had cough drops the next day— one each—because cough drops were as good as candy and just as pretty.

The little Teddy Bear fell on his face, and his
nose began to bleed hot red Teddy-Bear blood.
"Mother, Mother, I am sick
Call for the Doctor, quick, quick, quick."

Doctor Squash came running with his little bag. He told the little Teddy Bear to lie down. He put a piece of paper under his upper lip and a cold cloth on his forehead, and he held his paw.

Soon the nosebleed was over, and the Teddy Bear washed his face and went to sleep.

The Rag Doll couldn't whistle. She had eaten a green persimmon and she couldn't whistle.

So they sent for Doctor Squash.

"Say 'Ahhh,'" said Doctor Squash.

"Ahhh, Ahhh," said the Rag Doll.

Doctor Squash flashed his little flashlight at the Rag Doll's tonsils and up her nose.

"No sore throat," pronounced Doctor Squash. "You have been eating green persimmons. There is nothing now to do but wait. And next year wait two weeks before you eat them. Wait until the persimmons fall off the tree."

The little Fireman Doll broke his leg. The ladder broke. And the little Fireman fell down and broke his leg.

They telephoned the Doctor. Doctor Squash's car was broken. So they sent the fire engine to get him and he came rushing—with all the whistles blowing.

"How is your knee jerk?" asked the Doctor, tapping the Fireman's knee.

"It doesn't," said the Fireman.

It didn't jerk because it was broken.

"Get me a board as long as a leg," said Doctor Squash. And he took out rolls, and rolls, and rolls of white bandages from his black bag. And some adhesive tape, and scissors, and a bright, sharp knife.

They brought him the board, and he began to whittle. He whittled it smooth, and he whittled it clean. He whittled the splinters and the rough, sharp edges. And he whittled it just the length of the Fireman's leg, from knee to foot. And gently he tied it on. This was called a splint.

"You're all right now," said Doctor Squash. "Stay away from fires for three weeks. Then you'll be all right again— 'Fit as a fiddle and right as rain.'"

Then the little Clown caught measles. And not only that! He caught mumps, chicken pox, and whooping cough all at once. What a clown!

He looked funny in his clown pajamas. But he didn't feel funny, poor little Clown. He was spotted and puffed, and he tickled and he whooped.

Doctor Squash said, "I must make you well. But it will take time. At least two weeks."

And he wrote a prescription:

For measles - keep room dark
For mumps - stay very quiet
For chicken pox - don't scratch
For whooping - cough medicine
cough

Signed Doctor Squash

Then he put a big sign on the Clown's house that said:

And he sent the little Clown lots of oranges and grapes and toys to keep him busy until he could play with the other dolls again. And he sent him an apple a day.

The Indian Doll fell off his horse when he was out for a ride one day.

He fell among some shiny three-leaved plants. And all of a sudden he began to itch.

Poison Ivy!

Call for Doctor Squash!

Over the telephone Doctor Squash said, "Wash quickly! Brown laundry soap! I'll be over when the sun goes down."

Doctor Squash arrived with two big bottles of pink poison-ivy lotion.

The Indian Doll didn't have much poison ivy because he had washed so quickly with brown soap.

"But enough is enough," said Doctor Squash. "Put on the lotion. Don't scratch. And stay away from poison ivy!"

The winter came. As it got colder and longer, all the dolls started coughing. The cough drops didn't do any good.

"Say 'Ahhh,'" said Doctor Squash.

And then he swabbed their throats, and listened to their chests, and sprayed their noses, and looked in their eyes, and took their temperatures, and gave them green pills, and peppermint tea. And he made them some raw onion juice by slicing raw onions and putting sugar on them. And they each had a spoonful.

Soon they all felt better.

"Keep warm," said Doctor Squash. "And drink lots of water."

The next day he came back and gave them all inoculations for distemper and influenza.

"It will only hurt a little," said Doctor Squash.

All the dolls were brave.

It didn't hurt much more than a mosquito bite.

And the dolls stayed well for the rest of the winter.

But one dark day—

The Doctor was sick.

Poor Doctor Squash was sick.
He lay on the ground and howled, "Ow, ow."
All the dolls came running.

They opened his bag. And they took out a spoon and a bottle and some cotton and a flashlight and a stethoscope. And they made him lemonade.

One doll felt his head. Another took his temperature.
The Teddy Bear flashed the flashlight in his throat.
The Clown tried to make him laugh.

And the Fireman Doll tapped his knees to see if they jerked.

And they all listened through the stethoscope to his big warm pounding heart.

Of course, they couldn't hear it, because dolls can't hear. But they pretended they could to make him feel better. And they told him he would soon be "Fit as a fiddle and right as rain."

The Rag Doll counted his pulse.

"You have the pulse of an ox," she said, to make him feel stronger. Of course, she didn't know it, but she was right. He did. He had the pulse of an ox. And so he got well right away. Because all the dolls took such good care of him.

And now Doctor Squash is well again. His strength is as the strength of ten, and . . .

Whenever you are sick,
Call for the Doctor,
Quick, quick, quick.